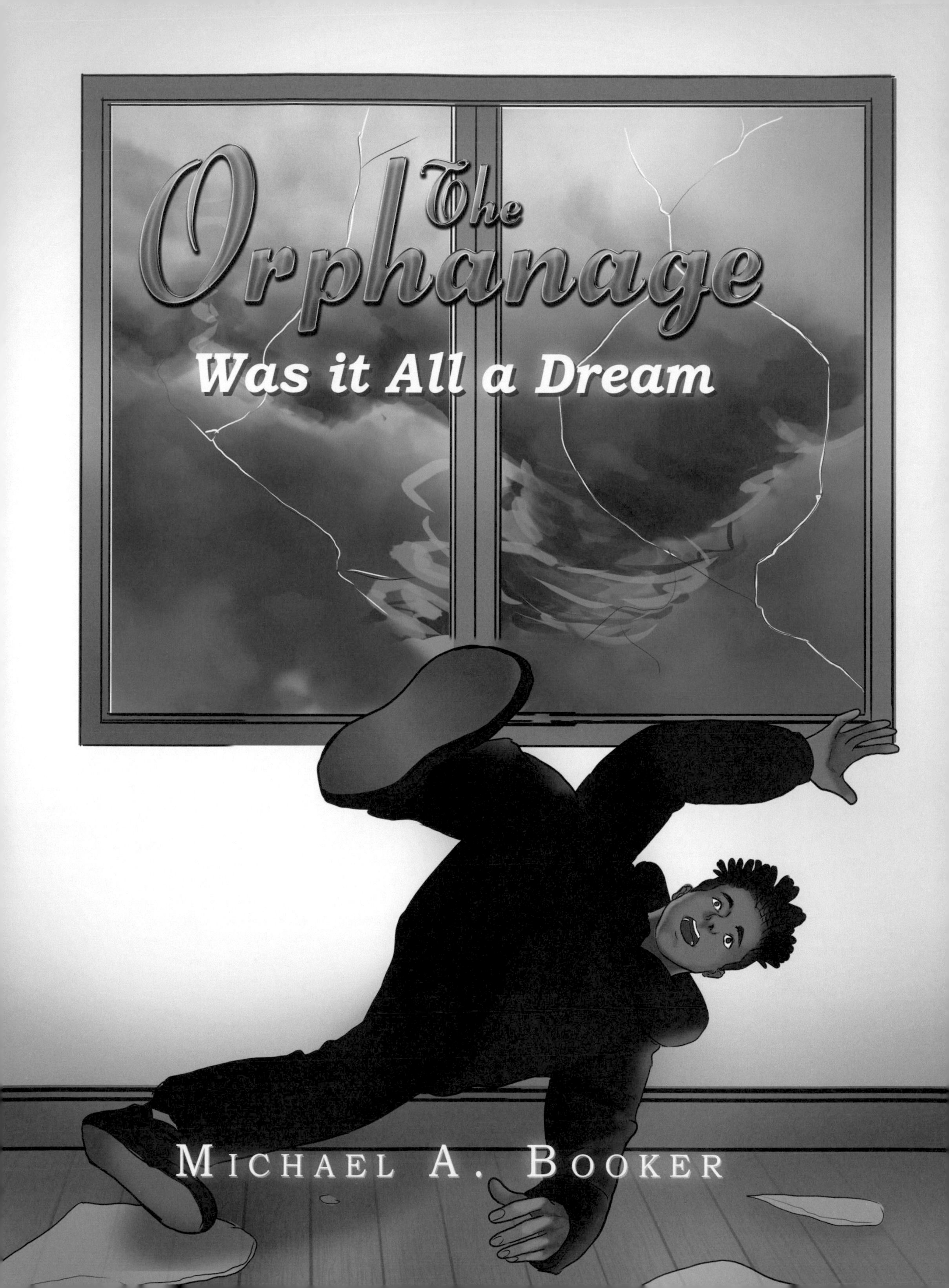
The Orphanage
Was it All a Dream
MICHAEL A. BOOKER

To order additional copies of this book, contact:
Xlibris
844-714-8691
www.Xlibris.com
Orders@Xlibris.com

ISBN:   Softcover        979-8-3694-1292-3
        EBook            979-8-3694-1291-6
Library of Congress Control Number:        2023923499
Print information available on the last page

Rev. date: 12/07/2023

# Contents

# Chapter 1

## A Day at the Orphanage

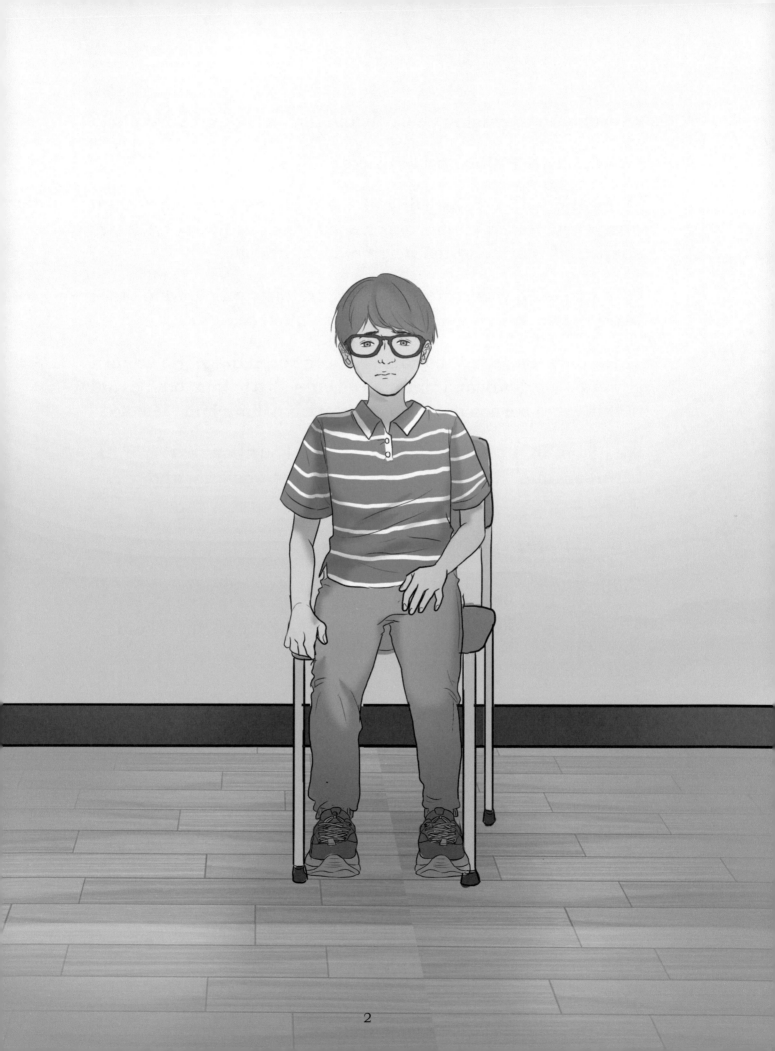

*I* woke up to ringing bells. "Wake up," yelled our caretaker.

"Why so early?" the new kid asked.

Mark and I have been living at the orphanage for more than two years. Based on our experience of boys talking back, we suspected that he would be greeted with a slap.

Our suspicion was correct, as our caretaker yelled, "don't talk back to me," and a slap came across his face.

Three days ago, a new boy arrived at the orphanage. He seemed shy but rude. Mark and I introduced ourselves to him, but he said nothing and turned away. So, we started calling him "The Kid."

We all got in a line to brush our teeth. Four boys can use the bathroom at a time as there are four sinks, showers, and toilets in there.

"The Kid" was sniffing from the slap.

I talked to my friend, Mark, quietly.

I bet you one quarter he is going to the white room," I said.

"Bet," he said.

About two minutes later The Kid was snatched up by the arm, his screams grabbed everyone's attention. He yelled, "Not the white room!

A shiver went down my spine as Mark gave me a quarter for winning the bet. If you don't know what the white room is, it's like a room in an inpatient psychiatric ward, or a mental health facility with all white pillows surrounding you.

Our second caretaker, Ms. Daisy, who is nice, went into the room. We could hear arguing. The Kid came out of the room screaming and hid under his bed.

About a minute later, Ms. Daisy came out to let us know that breakfast would be soon.

She went back into the room, and we could hear more arguing.

She walked out the room saying, "This is unacceptable, Ms. Gribble," which is the name of our mean caretaker who had put The Kid in the white room.

Ms. Daisy sat down and yelled cheerfully, "Huddle up children."

After we brushed our teeth, she sang us a song. Then we got ready for breakfast. Luckily, she cooked us eggs, grits, bacon, and sausage.

After breakfast, we had free time, but it was interrupted by Kim yelling, "Tooth, I found a tooth!" Everyone came running to try and take the tooth away from him. Mark, two of the other boys, and I stared as Ms. Daisy stopped Josh and Charlie from taking the tooth away from Kim.

Some of us were rewarded with candy for not getting involved. After a while everything settled down. The reason everyone freaked out about the tooth was because if you sleep with one underneath your pillow, you will be given some coins. This is the only time when we are given money to buy candy.

Ms. Daisy gave us a speech on how we should not fight because someone could get hurt. But not too long later, one of the boys raised his hand. He yelled, "What if we pulled out our teeth?"

Five boys ran to their pillows, pulled out a string from it and ran into the bathroom. A few minutes later, we heard screaming. Two boys ran out with a mouth full of blood and a tooth in hand. Ms. Daisy was able to stop the other three boys from pulling out their teeth. She found out they were using the string from their pillows to saw their teeth out, just for a couple of coins.

# Chapter 2

## Tooth Trouble

The next day the boys who saw their teeth out got the coins and the candy they so desperately wanted. The rest of us just stared at each other and shook our heads at the sadness of it all.

Leo stayed in the bathroom claiming he needed to use it. We could see more boys going back to the bathroom.

At first, we ignored it because we were already at the table eating. Soon, they came out of the bathroom three of them with a tooth in hand and a bunch of bloody toilet paper in their mouths. Ms. Daisy screamed and quickly took them to her office. Ms. Gribble then came out looking grumpier than ever and carrying a sheet of paper in her hand.

"Charlie," she yelled.

"Yes, Ms. Gribble" he said.

"Your adopted parents are here! Go outside, Mr. and Mrs. Jamison are waiting for you."

Within a blink of an eye, he ran out of the room, turned, and said goodbye, excited for his new life.

We ran to the window and watched as Charlie hugged his new parents and watched as the new family drove away.

"Lucky," Mark said, clearly upset.

"Don't worry, Mark. One day wc will be adopted," I said.

"Hopefully soon," he said.

Ms. Gribble then stepped back into her office. And at the same time, Ms. Daisy came out of the office. I asked if the boys were OK. She replied, "They need to go to the hospital. The ambulance is coming—do not be alarmed."

We all looked at each other in silence, but soon sirens broke the quiet. Ms. Daisy went to meet the ambulance, with five boys running behind her and out the front door. Mr. Carter, our counselor, went to the hospital with the boys.

Ten minutes later, Ms. Daisy walked back in, trying to hold her smile and lift her head up, but clearly that was hard to do. She went into her office, and we heard her crying. We all felt sorry for Ms. Daisy, and we sat on our beds, not knowing what to do.

Ms. Gribble walked out screaming, "Who made Ms. Daisy cry?"

Josh said, "some of the boys pulled out one of their teeth and had to be taken to the hospital because their gums wouldn't stop bleeding."

Ms. Gribble then felt sorry for Ms. Daisy. She went into Ms. Daisy's office to comfort her. A few of us walked to Ms. Daisy's office door to eavesdrop.

# Chapter 3

# The Talk

We heard Ms. Gribble talking, but we could only make out some of the words because their voices where muffled. "I know you're sad, but we still have other things to worry about," she said.

After about five more minutes of them talking, we heard footsteps coming toward the door. We ran to our bedroom as Ms. Gribble came out the door.

"OK children, off to bed, she said."

"Where's Ms. Daisy?" The Kid asked.

She walked over and pulled him by the ear, and yelled, "Don't talk back to me!"

Mark bet twenty-five cents he was going to the white room. This time, I hesitated but still agreed to the bet.

The next day, Ms. Daisy woke us up and told us to line up to brush our teeth. While we were in line The Kid was punished again for talking back last night. This time, he was sent to the silent room.

"What's the silent room again?" asked Mark.

"The silent room is completely dark. And you are stuck in there for two hours without food or water," I said.

"Oh, right," Mark said, "I had forgotten about the silent room because no one has been sent there for a long time." Again, Mark lost the bet and handed me twenty-five cents, as I stared at the silent room entrance.

Meanwhile, Ms. Daisy looked like she had cried all night and didn't get any sleep. She cried a lot, and I mean a lot! There were bags under her eyes, and she looked droopy. She was not her cheerful self at all. She treated us like we were her own children, but today she barely looked at us.

We continued with our day studying and doing chores. But all day long something felt off—different. Suddenly a loud boom sounded in the distance, and then a window shattered as a strong gust of wind came flying toward me. Within a second everything went black. I woke up to chaos. People were screaming, tanks were erupting, and police cars were rushing across the now destroyed city. Mark and I jumped up, clearly scared for our lives. The front of the building was broken open, and a gaping hole allowed us to see what was going on.

**Chapter 4**

# An Attack?

We ran out of the orphanage to seek shelter. People were stealing and robbing people, and helicopters were everywhere. People were killing other people with knifes, guns, sticks—you name it. The military was sent to help, but they were even being attacked. Turns out a huge mental health facility was blown up by a military attack helicopter that was stolen from a military base.

The explosion had damaged many of the buildings in the area—even the prison, and all the prisoners had escaped. I found this out when I stopped running to listen to the news broadcasting in the TV shop next door to the orphanage.

"Hurry up Maxwell, Mark said running alongside Kim, Josh, and The Kid. Run so we can live, man! I don't want to leave without you, Mark said.

But I turned and I ran back to the orphanage to save the others trapped in the debris. After saving all of the other boys trapped inside, I told them to wait there while I looked for Ms. Daisy. I found her and saved her too.

She asked, "Did you save the other boys?

"Yes," I said, "the mean caretaker only saved herself."

"Wc must find shelter," said Ms. Daisy.

After running inside a nearby underground parking garage, we concluded that we had to stock up on supplies. So, we raided stores, getting first aid kits, food, water, and a TV because we needed to know what was going on. And we needed entertainment. (This was my idea). After setting everything up, we huddled up and watched the news to see more.

"Maxwell, "turn on the TV," quick!" Josh said.

"OK," I said.

After switching through different news channels, it turns out all the prisoners had broken out of prison because of the explosion that caused all the chaos that was going on.

"Oh no..." I was quickly cut off by Kim.

What's that? He asked. Once we spotted the black figure in the distance, it began to run towards all of us. It had long arms, and its mouth was wide open. Everyone screamed. And then I woke up, horrified! I could not move; I was too scared. Then, I heard the sound of running water coming from the sink, kids getting out of bed, and people talking.

I got out of bed. I asked myself, Was that a dream or real?

## Chapter 5

# Was it all a Dream?

*I* got up and everything was fine. Was I dreaming? I thought. I got in line to brush my teeth. I asked Mark what happened.

He said, "You just fell to the floor and began to sweat a lot. You did not look good at all. You looked scared. And man, you blacked out after you looked out the window."

"Wait—wait—what?" I stuttered. "How?"

"They called the doctor, and he said it is not a problem, and you are fine. It may be a virus or food poisoning."

Ms. Daisy came out of her office and spoke. "Good news children! The boys have made a full recovery. Oh, and it looks like you made a full recovery too, Maxwell."

"Yes, I did," I said.

We then all cheered. I was happy we were alive. And I was OK. Ms. Daisy was happy again. But still, the same thought pondered in my mind. Was it all a dream?

## To Be Continued

Printed in the United States
by Baker & Taylor Publisher Services